This Pokémon Annual belongs to:

....

I am: .... **years old**

My Pokémon Buddy is:

....

Farshore

First published in Great Britain 2021 by Farshore
An imprint of HarperCollins*Publishers*
1 London Bridge Street, London SE1 9GF
www.farshore.co.uk

HarperCollins*Publishers*
1st Floor, Watermarque Building, Ringsend Road, Dublin 4, Ireland

Written by Emily Stead. Edited by Katrina Pallant.
Designed by Grant Kempster. Cover designed by Jessica Coomber.

ISBN 978 0 7555 0111 3
Printed in Romania
004

A CIP catalogue record for this book is available from the British Library.

POKÉMON™

ANNUAL 2022

CONTENTS

GREETINGS FROM GALAR!

On the next part of his journey to become a Pokémon Master, Ash must leave his home in Pallet Town and travel to Galar, the latest known region in the world of Pokémon! Equipped with a Rotom Phone, Ash can scan each new Pokémon that he discovers.

In this Annual, you can read about Ash's adventures in the Galar region and meet some new and exciting Pokémon yourself in the Galar A–Z. Complete the activities and puzzles to raise your Trainer game!

"NO TIME TO WASTE – THE JOURNEY STARTS TODAY!"

JOINING THE JOURNEY

Ash meets new friends Goh and Chloe when he takes a trip to Vermilion City. While Goh can't wait to discover new species of Pokémon, Chloe is more cautious when she encounters creatures for the first time.

FACT FILE

Name: Goh
Age: 10
Lives: Vermilion City, Kanto
Pokémon: A Scorbunny, which evolves into a Raboot, then a Cinderace!
About: Goh hates homework – he'd rather study Pokémon! He dreams of catching Mew, while his ultimate goal is to complete his Pokédex.

FACT FILE

Name: Chloe
Age: 10
Lives: Vermilion City, Kanto
Pokémon: Chloe's family pet is a Yamper, while her first Pokémon was an Eevee.
About: She is the daughter of Professor Cerise, the head of the Cerise Laboratory in Vermilion City. Chloe is nervous around new Pokémon.

SPOT THE DIFFERENCE

1

2

Ash and Goh are two Trainers who are ready for adventure! Find 8 differences between the pictures above.

The answers are on page 69.

BRIGHT SPARK

Trace the paths and write the letters below to reveal a Pokémon that's a real live wire! Use the picture clues to help you!

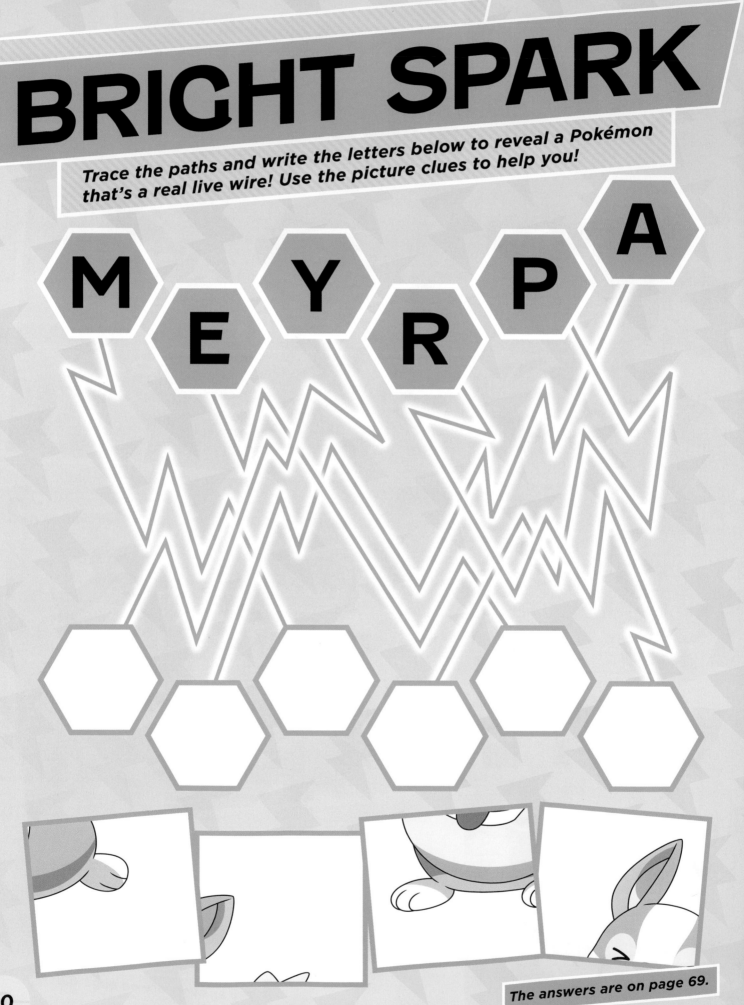

The answers are on page 69.

ON THE GOH!

Discovering Pokémon is Goh's favourite hobby! Guide him through the Wild Area maze to meet the Mythical Mew, passing new faces Grookey and Scorbunny along the way!

START

FINISH

The answers are on page 69.

PERFECT POKÉ BALLS

Ash only has one of each type of Poké Ball.
Which one should he use to give him the best chance
to catch all four of the Pokémon below?
Connect the Pokémon to the right
Poké Ball each time.

BUTTERFREE

MEW

The Dive Ball works well when catching underwater Pokémon.

As day turns to night, a host of Pokémon come out to play. Smart Trainers keep supplies of Dusk Balls to hand.

The Net Ball will give a Trainer greater success when catching Bug-type Pokémon.

GENGAR

Save the Master Ball to make a Legendary catch or to snare a Mythical Pokémon.

GRENINJA

The answers are on page 69.

FIRING UP

Start at number 1, then join the dots in order to reveal which flying fire-breather is blazing a trail through Galar's skies.

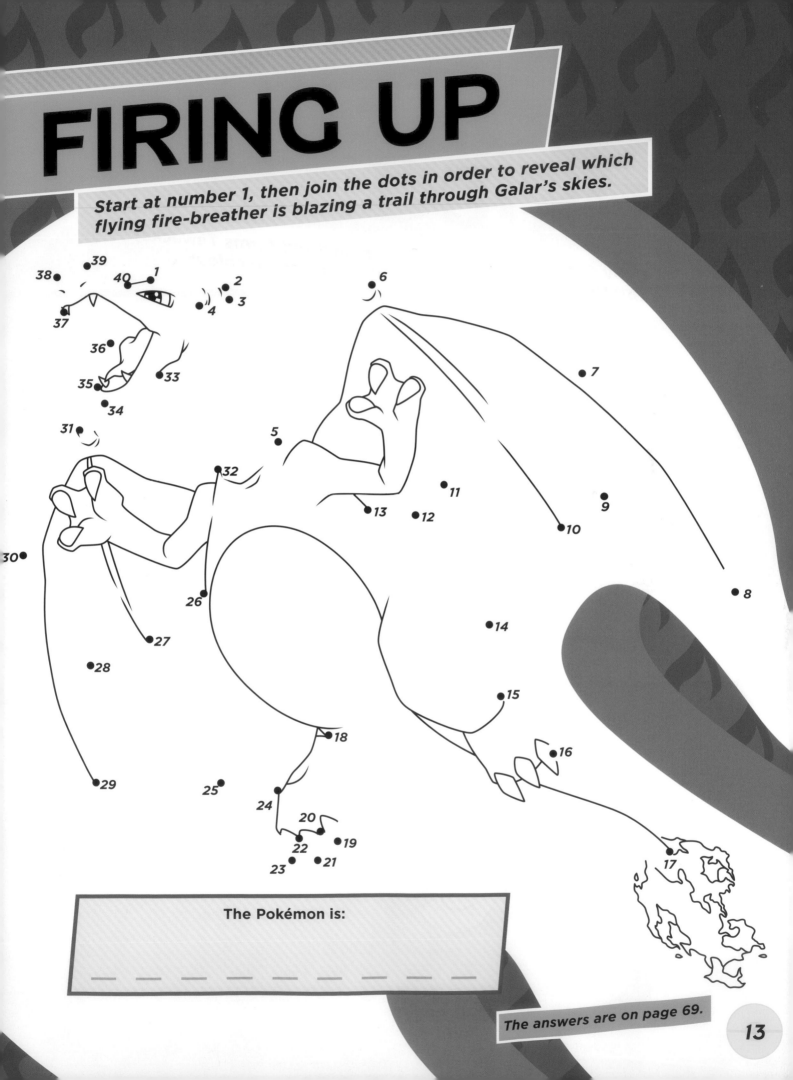

The Pokémon is:

_ _ _ _ _ _ _ _ _

The answers are on page 69.

13

GROOKEY'S GRIDS

Copy Grass-type Grookey and its evolved forms Thwackey and Rillaboom into the grids, then add some colour.

The sound waves produced by the beat of Grookey's stick carry energy to nearby flowers and plants.

Thwackey
can beat out a
rapid rhythm
with its two
sticks.

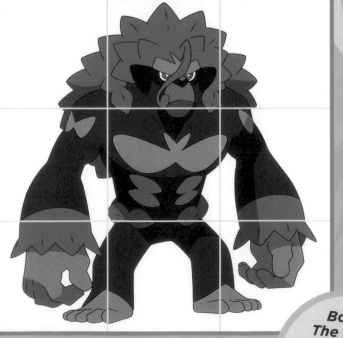

Boom!
The sound
of Rillaboom's
drumming can
be heard
throughout
the forest.

LEGEND? GO! FRIENDS? GO!

*A*nother day, another late start! If Ash wants to become a Pokémon Master, he's going to have to set his alarm. After all, the early Trainer catches the Pokémon!

After sleeping in again, Ash and Pikachu had to run all the way to meet Professor Oak on time. Ash arrived at the lab, red-faced.

"Ah, Ash!" the professor replied. "A friend of mine has just opened a brand new research lab in Vermilion City. I'd like to invite you to the opening ceremony. You will come, won't you?"

"Sure!" smiled Ash. "You'll come too, right Pikachu?"

"I'd love to!" a voice behind them interrupted. It was Ash's mother, Delia. She and Mr Mime had brought Ash's packed lunch. "All those fancy shops to visit . . ."

Ash shrugged. He could see that his mum had her mind made up. So moments later, they all set off for Vermilion City.

A couple of hours later, they arrived at the Cerise Laboratory. Ash, Pikachu and Professor Oak went inside for the ceremony, while Delia headed to the nearest shops!

"Welcome to the Cerise Research Laboratory," a man in a lab coat announced. "I am Professor Cerise."

Ash's eyes were wide with wonder.

"The team here studies Pokémon in every region," Professor Cerise went on. "We investigate and dig deep to expand our knowledge, because to know Pokémon is to know the world!"

The audience began to clap and cheer.

Just then, an alert flashed up on the lab's enormous video screen. Professor Oak and Professor Cerise studied the data together.

"Let's see," said Professor Cerise. "The latest temperature, humidity and altitude readings suggest that an extremely rare Pokémon may appear at the port, very soon!"

"A rare Pokémon?" Ash gasped. This was too good to be true! So he and Pikachu slipped out of the lab to check out the possible appearance.

Meanwhile, another Trainer was waiting at the port for a glimpse of the rare Pokémon. His name was Goh, and his mission was to catch every Pokémon in every region, a task almost as impossible as his second goal – catching a *Mythical Mew!*

So when the Legendary Lugia showed up in the skies above the city, Goh took a leap of faith and jumped on to its tail.

"Don't leave without me, Lugia!" Goh called. He was hanging on for dear life!

Moments later, Lugia picked up more passengers, when Ash and Pikachu hitched a ride on the Pokémon, too! When Goh crawled up Lugia's tail, the two Trainers came face to face.

"How did *you* get here?" gasped Goh and Ash at the same time.

The Pokémon swooped and swirled in the skies, with the boys clinging on as tightly as they could. Eventually, Lugia slowed to a gentler speed, allowing Ash and Goh to catch their breath.

"What an amazing ride!" cried Ash.

Goh used his Rotom Phone to record every detail of the fascinating flyer, from the way its fins moved to the texture of its feathers.

Suddenly, Lugia soared high again, into position at the head of a flock of Fearow.

"What incredible flying power!" Goh marvelled.

But their rollercoaster ride on-board Lugia wasn't over – as Lugia plunged headfirst towards the ocean waves below!

Before hitting the water, Ash, Goh and Pikachu all took a deep breath. Lugia's underwater tour was about to begin! So many weird and wonderful Water Pokémon swam up to say hello – from a fearsome Cloyster to a whole school of Shellder! Ash couldn't wait to tell Professor Cerise!

Then, just as the boys and Pikachu were running out of breath, Lugia rose gracefully out of the water again.

"That was close!" Goh panted.

Ash smiled. "But worth it to meet all those awesome Pokémon!"

Goh laughed. "You're pretty funny, you know?" he said. "So I've decided something . . . that you're going to be my friend!"

It was time for some proper intros. "I'm Goh, from Vermillion City."

"I'm Ash, from Pallet Town," Ash replied. "And this is Pikachu."

Moments later, Lugia decided that the Trainers' journey had come to an end. It swooped low, ahead of a family of fiery-maned Rapidash, before tossing its passengers from its back.

They landed in a grassy meadow with a **bump!**

"Lugia may be Legendary, but it's no Ride Pokémon!" said Ash. They waved goodbye, as Lugia flapped its mighty wings and soared into the distance.

"Pokémon really are the coolest, huh?" sighed Ash happily.

Goh smiled. "Yes, Lugia made me really think about things," he began. "There's a **whole world** out there to explore, if that's what you truly desire."

"No doubt about it!" Ash agreed, raising his hand for a high-five.

"Come on, Ash," said Goh, dusting himself down. "It's time we got back."

"One problem," Ash replied, looking around. "Which way *is* back?"

By the time the three adventurers reached the city and Professor Cerise's lab, the sun was setting.

As usual, the professor was working late. He was amazed when Goh shared the shots of Lugia on Goh's Rotom Phone. "I've never seen such close-ups," Professor Cerise gasped. "Lugia's back fins in full flight and clear as day!"

"Wait 'til you see the ones we took underwater!" Goh beamed.

The professor turned to Ash. "How was your experience?" he asked.

"You know, for a little while, it felt like we actually became friends with Lugia," Ash smiled.

"PIKA!" Pikachu agreed.

"When my eyes met Lugia's, shivers went down my spine," Ash explained. "And just before we hit the water, I heard a voice saying 'Here we go!'"

The professor gasped. He was so impressed with Ash and Goh for everything they had discovered about the Legendary Pokémon. It was time for the boys' reward.

The professor cleared his throat. "It's because of you two that I've learned things about Lugia that no one has ever known!" he began. "So I have a request . . ."

Goh and Ash looked at each other and shrugged. Neither knew what the professor was going to say next.

"Would you do me the honour of becoming research assistants in my new lab?" Professor Cerise smiled.

"*Woah!* What would that job involve?" asked Ash.

"You'll get to meet all kinds of Pokémon," the professor explained. "Share thoughts and ideas as a team, and help with our important Pokémon studies!"

"That's music to my ears!" Goh smiled.

"Then I'll do it, too!" Ash added.

And so it was settled. Ash and Goh became Professor Cerise's newest research assistants, ready to do whatever it took to discover and protect Pokémon in every region.

It was a big responsibility – Ash would have to move to the city and share a room with his new friend, Goh. The only matter left to be decided? You guessed it – who would get the top bunk!

Meeting the Legendary Lugia that day opened Ash and Goh's eyes to a world full of dreams, adventure and of course, Pokémon. Which creatures will they meet next? The journey continues!

THE PROFESSOR'S QUIZ

Professor Cerise has set you a quiz to test your knowledge of the powerful Pokémon, Lugia! How will you score?

1 Is Lugia a Legendary or a Mythical Pokémon?

Legendary ☐   *Mythical* ☐

2 Tick the boxes to show Lugia's correct type category.

Flying ☐   *Fairy* ☐   *Water* ☐   *Psychic* ☐

3 Can Lugia swim?

Yes ☐   *No* ☐

4 Does Lugia evolve from or into another Pokémon?

Yes ☐   *No* ☐

5 How tall is mighty Lugia?

1.5 m ☐   *3.6 m* ☐   *5.2 m* ☐

6 Which part of Lugia packs devastating power?

Its jaws ☐   *Its talons* ☐   *Its wings* ☐

The answers are on page 69.

STRANGE SIGHTING

Following reports of a bunch of Ivysaur causing chaos in the City Park, Ash and Goh have been sent to investigate. Help them to catch 16 peeking Pokémon.

The answers are on page 69.

GALAR DISCOVERIES

Ash and Goh's adventures in Galar have seen them discover some rare and interesting creatures! Place the names of these Pokémon in their Galarian form in the grid below.

10 LETTERS
DARMANITAN

9 LETTERS
ZIGZAGOON

8 LETTERS
DARUMAKA
RAPIDASH
STUNFISK

7 LETTERS
CORSOLA
LINOONE
WEEZING

6 LETTERS
MEOWTH
PONYTA
MR MIME
YAMASK

Tip: try to fit the longer words first!

The answers are on page 69.

GALAR A-Z

Ash and Goh are having a blast exploring the Galar region together! Check out some of the Pokémon that they might be lucky enough to run into on their travels – from familiar faces to rare Legendary creatures! All the data is recorded on their Rotom Phones.

ALCREMIE

Fairy
0.3 m
0.5 kg

About: When it trusts a Trainer, it will treat them to berries it's decorated with cream.

APPLETUN

Grass • Dragon
0.4 m
13.0 kg

About: Its body is covered in sweet nectar, and the skin on its back is especially yummy. Children used to have it as a snack.

APPLIN

Grass • Dragon
0.2 m
0.5 kg

About: It spends its entire life inside an apple. It hides from its natural enemies, bird Pokémon, by pretending it's just an apple and nothing more.

ARAQUANID

Water • Bug
1.8 m
82.0 kg

About: It acts as a caretaker for Dewpider, putting them inside its bubble and letting them eat any leftover food.

ARCANINE

Fire
1.9 m
155.0 kg

About: The sight of it running over 6200 miles in a single day and night has captivated many people.

ARCTOVISH

Water • Ice
2.0 m
175.0 kg

About: Though it's able to capture prey by freezing its surroundings, it has trouble eating the prey afterwards because its mouth is on top of its head.

ARCTOZOLT

Electric • Ice
2.3 m
150.0 kg

About: This Pokémon lived on prehistoric seashores and was able to preserve food with the ice on its body. It went extinct because it moved so slowly.

ARROKUDA

Water
0.5 m
1.0 kg

About: If it sees any movement around it, this Pokémon charges for it straight away, leading with its sharply pointed jaw. It's very proud of that jaw.

BARRASKEWDA

Water
1.3 m
30.0 kg

About: This Pokémon has a jaw that's as sharp as a spear and as strong as steel. Apparently Barraskewda's flesh is surprisingly tasty, too.

BOLTUND

Electric
1.0 m
34.0 kg

About: This Pokémon generates electricity and channels it into its legs to keep them going strong. Boltund can run non-stop for three full days.

BRAVIARY

Normal • Flying
1.5 m
41.0 kg

About: Known for its bravery and pride, this majestic Pokémon is often seen as a motif for various kinds of emblems.

BUTTERFREE

Bug • Flying
1.1 m
32.0 kg

About: In battle, it flaps its wings at great speed to release highly toxic dust into the air.

CENTISKORCH

Fire • Bug
3.0 m
120.0 kg

About: While its burning body is already dangerous on its own, this excessively hostile Pokémon also has large and very sharp fangs.

CHARIZARD

Fire • Flying
1.7 m
90.5 kg

About: It spits fire that is hot enough to melt boulders. It may cause forest fires by blowing flames.

CHARJABUG

Bug • Electric
0.5 m
10.5 kg

About: While its durable shell protects it from attacks, Charjabug strikes at enemies with jolts of electricity discharged from the tips of its jaws.

CHARMANDER

Fire
0.6 m
8.5 kg

About: It has a preference for hot things. When it rains, steam is said to spout from the tip of its tail.

CHARMELEON

Fire
1.1 m
19.0 kg

About: It has a barbaric nature. In battle, it whips its fiery tail around and slashes away with sharp claws.

CLOBBOPUS

Fighting
0.6 m
4.0 kg

About: Its tentacles tear off easily, but it isn't alarmed when that happens – it knows they'll grow back. It's about as smart as a three year-old.

COALOSSAL

Rock • Fire
2.8 m
310.5 kg

About: While it's engaged in battle, its mountain of coal will burn bright red, sending off sparks that scorch the surrounding area.

COPPERAJAH

Steel
3.0 m
650.0 kg

About: These Pokémon live in herds. Their trunks have incredible grip strength, strong enough to crush giant rocks into powder.

GALARIAN CORSOLA

Ghost
0.6 m
0.5 kg

About: Sudden climate change wiped out this ancient kind of Corsola. This Pokémon absorbs others' life-force through its branches.

CORVIKNIGHT

Flying • Steel
2.2 m
75.0 kg

About: With their great intellect and flying skills, these Pokémon very successfully act as the Galar region's airborne taxi service.

CORVISQUIRE

Flying
0.8 m
16.0 kg

About: Smart enough to use tools in battle, these Pokémon have been seen picking up rocks and flinging them or using ropes to wrap up enemies.

CUFANT

Steel
1.2 m
100.0 kg

About: If a job requires serious strength, this Pokémon will excel at it. Its copper body tarnishes in the rain, turning a vibrant green colour.

CURSOLA

Ghost
1.0 m
0.4 kg

About: Be cautious of the ectoplasmic body surrounding its soul. You'll become stiff as stone if you touch it.

GALARIAN DARMANITAN

Ice
1.7 m
120.0 kg

About: On days when blizzards blow through, it comes down to where people live. It stashes food in the snowball on its head, taking it home for later.

GALARIAN DARUMAKA

Ice
0.7 m
40.0 kg

About: It lived in snowy areas for so long that its fire sac cooled off and atrophied. It now has an organ that generates cold instead.

DEINO

Dark • Dragon
0.8 m
17.3 kg

About: Because it can't see, this Pokémon is constantly biting at everything it touches, trying to keep track of its surroundings.

DEWPIDER

Water • Bug
0.3 m
4.0 kg

About: Dewpider normally lives underwater. When it comes onto land in search of food, it takes water with it in the form of a bubble on its head.

DOTTLER

Bug • Psychic
0.4 m
19.5 kg

About: It barely moves, but it's still alive. Hiding in its shell without food or water seems to have awakened its psychic powers.

DRACOVISH

Water • Dragon
2.3 m
215.0 kg

About: Its mighty legs are capable of running at speeds exceeding 40 mph, but this Pokémon can't breathe unless it's underwater.

DRACOZOLT

Electric • Dragon
1.8 m
190.0 kg

About: The powerful muscles in its tail generate its electricity. Compared to its lower body, its upper half is entirely too small.

DRAGAPULT

Dragon • Ghost
3.0 m
50.0 kg

About: When it isn't battling, it keeps Dreepy in the holes on its horns. Once a fight starts, it launches the Dreepy like supersonic missiles.

DRAKLOAK

Dragon • Ghost
1.4 m
11.0 kg

About: It's capable of flying faster than 120 mph. It battles alongside Dreepy and dotes on them until they successfully evolve.

DRAMPA

Normal • Dragon
3.0 m
185.0 kg

About: The mountains it calls home are nearly two miles in height. On rare occasions, it descends to play with the children living in the towns below.

DREDNAW

Water • Rock
1.0 m
115.5 kg

About: With jaws that can shear through steel rods, this highly aggressive Pokémon chomps down on its unfortunate prey.

DREEPY

Dragon • Ghost
0.5 m
2.0 kg

About: After being reborn as a ghost Pokémon, Dreepy wanders the areas it used to inhabit back when it was alive in prehistoric seas.

DUBWOOL

Normal
1.3 m
43.0 kg

About: Weave a carpet from its springy wool, and you end up with something closer to a trampoline. You'll start to bounce the moment you set foot on it.

DURALUDON

Steel • Dragon
1.8 m
40.0 kg

About: The special metal that composes its body is very light, so this Pokémon has considerable agility. It lives in caves because it dislikes the rain.

DUSCLOPS

Ghost
1.6 m
30.6 kg

About: Its body is entirely hollow. When it opens its mouth, it sucks everything in as if it were a black hole.

DUSKNOIR

Ghost
2.2 m
106.6 kg

About: With the mouth on its belly, Dusknoir swallows its target whole. The soul is the only thing eaten – Dusknoir disgorges the body before departing.

DUSKULL

Ghost
0.8 m
15.0 kg

About: Making itself invisible, it silently sneaks up to prey. It has the ability to slip through thick walls.

EEVEE

Normal
0.3 m
6.5 kg

About: Thanks to its unstable genetic make-up, this special Pokémon conceals many different possible evolutions.

EISCUE

Ice
1.4 m
89.0 kg

About: This Pokémon keeps its heat-sensitive head cool with ice. It fishes for its food, dangling its single hair into the sea to lure in prey.

ELDEGOSS

Grass
0.5 m
2.5 kg

About: The cotton on the head of this Pokémon can be spun into a glossy, gorgeous yarn – a Galar regional speciality.

ESPEON

Psychic
0.9 m
26.5 kg

About: It unleashes psychic power from the orb on its forehead. When its power is exhausted, the orb grows dull and dark.

ESPURR

Psychic
0.3 m
3.5 kg

About: There's enough psychic power in Espurr to send a wrestler flying, but because this power can't be controlled, Espurr finds it troublesome.

ETERNATUS *LEGENDARY*

Poison • Dragon
20.0 m
950.0 kg

About: The core on its chest absorbs energy emanating from the lands of the Galar region. This energy is what allows Eternatus to stay active.

FALINKS

Fighting
3.0 m
62.0 kg

About: The six of them work together as one Pokémon. Teamwork is also their battle strategy, and they constantly change their formation as they fight.

GALARIAN FARFETCH'D

Fighting
0.8 m
42.0 kg

About: The Farfetch'd of the Galar region are brave warriors, and they wield thick, tough leeks in battle.

FEEBAS

Water
0.6 m
7.4 kg

About: It is a shabby and ugly Pokémon. However, it is very hardy and can survive on little water.

FLAPPLE

Grass • Dragon
0.3 m
1.0 kg

About: It flies on wings of apple skin and spits a powerful acid. It can also change its shape into that of an apple.

FLAREON

Fire
0.9 m
25.0 kg

About: It stores some of the air it inhales in its internal flame pouch, which heats it to almost 150 degrees Celsius.

FROSMOTH

Ice • Bug
1.3 m
42.0 kg

About: It shows no mercy to any who desecrate fields and mountains. It will fly around on its icy wings, causing a blizzard to chase offenders away.

GALLADE

Psychic • Fighting
1.6 m
52.0 kg

About: Sharply attuned to others' wishes for help, this Pokémon seeks out those in need and aids them in battle.

GALVANTULA

Bug • Electric
0.8 m
14.3 kg

About: It lays traps of electrified threads near the nests of bird Pokémon, aiming to snare chicks that are not yet good at flying.

GARBODOR

Poison
1.9 m
107.3 kg

About: This Pokémon eats trash, which turns into poison inside its body. The main component of the poison depends on what sort of trash was eaten.

GARDEVOIR

Psychic • Fairy
1.6 m
48.4 kg

About: To protect its Trainer, it will expend all its psychic power to create a small black hole.

GASTLY

Ghost • Poison
1.3 m
0.1 kg

About: With its gas-like body, it can sneak into any place it desires. However, it can be blown away by wind.

GENGAR

Ghost • Poison
1.5 m
40.5 kg

About: On the night of a full moon, if shadows move on their own and laugh, it must be Gengar's doing.

GLACEON

Ice
0.8 m
25.9 kg

About: Any who become captivated by the beauty of the snowfall that Glaceon creates will be frozen before they know it.

GOSSIFLEUR

Grass
0.4 m
2.2 kg

About: It anchors itself in the ground with its single leg, then basks in the sun. After absorbing enough sunlight, its petals spread as it blooms brilliantly.

GRAPPLOCT

Fighting
1.6 m
39.0 kg

About: A body made up of nothing but muscle makes the grappling moves this Pokémon performs with its tentacles tremendously powerful.

GREEDENT

Normal
0.6 m
6.0 kg

About: Common throughout the Galar region, this Pokémon has strong teeth and can chew through the toughest of berry shells.

GRIMMSNARL

Dark • Fairy
1.5 m
61.0 kg

About: With the hair wrapped around its body helping to enhance its muscles, this Pokémon can overwhelm even Machamp.

GROOKEY

Grass
0.3 m
5.0 kg

About: It attacks with rapid beats of its stick. As it strikes with amazing speed, it gets more and more pumped.

GROWLITHE

Fire
0.7 m
19.0 kg

About: Extremely loyal, it will fearlessly bark at any opponent to protect its own Trainer from harm.

GRUBBIN

Bug
0.4 m
4.4 kg

About: It uses its big jaws to dig nests into the forest floor, and it loves to feed on sweet tree sap.

GYARADOS

Water • Flying
6.5 m
235.0 kg

About: Once it begins to rampage, a Gyarados will burn everything down, even in a harsh storm.

HAKAMO-O

Dragon • Fighting
1.2 m
47.0 kg

About: The scaleless, scarred parts of its body are signs of its strength. It shows them off to defeated opponents.

HATENNA

Psychic
0.4 m
3.4 kg

About: If this Pokémon senses a strong emotion, it will run away as fast as it can. It prefers areas without people.

HATTERENE

Psychic • Fairy
2.1 m
5.1 kg

About: If you're too loud around it, you risk being torn apart by the claws on its tentacle. This Pokémon is also known as the Forest Witch.

HATTREM

Psychic
0.6 m
4.8 kg

About: Using the braids on its head, it pummels foes to get them to quiet down. One blow from those braids would knock out a professional boxer.

HAUNTER

Ghost • Poison
1.6 m
0.1 kg

About: If you get the feeling of being watched in darkness when nobody is around, Haunter is there.

HAWLUCHA

Fighting • Flying
0.8 m
21.5 kg

About: It always strikes a pose before going for its finishing move. Sometimes opponents take advantage of that time to counter-attack.

HYDREIGON

Dark • Dragon
1.8 m
160.0 kg

About: There are a slew of stories about villages that were destroyed by Hydreigon. It bites anything that moves.

IMPIDIMP

Dark • Fairy
0.4 m
5.5 kg

About: It sneaks into people's homes, stealing things and feasting on the negative energy of the frustrated occupants.

INDEEDEE

Psychic • Normal
0.9 m
28.0 kg

About: Through its horns, it can pick up on the emotions of creatures around it. Positive emotions are the source of its strength.

INTELEON

Water
1.9 m
45.2 kg

About: It has many hidden capabilities, such as fingertips that can shoot water and a membrane on its back that it can use to glide through the air.

JANGMO-O

Dragon
0.6 m
29.7 kg

About: Jangmo-o strikes its scales to communicate with others of its kind. Its scales are actually fur that's become as hard as metal.

JOLTEON

Electric
0.8 m
24.5 kg

About: If it is angered or startled, the fur all over its body bristles like sharp needles that pierce foes.

JOLTIK

Bug • Electric
0.1 m
0.6 kg

About: Joltik latch on to other Pokémon and suck out static electricity. They're often found sticking to Yamper's hindquarters.

KIRLIA

Psychic • Fairy
0.8 m
20.2 kg

About: If its Trainer becomes happy, it overflows with energy, dancing joyously while spinning about.

KOMMO-O

Dragon • Fighting
1.6 m
78.2 kg

About: Certain ruins have paintings of ancient warriors wearing armour made of Kommo-o scales.

LAPRAS

Water • Ice
2.5 m
220.0 kg

About: A smart and kind-hearted Pokémon, it glides across the surface of the sea while its beautiful song echoes around it.

LEAFEON

Grass
1.0 m
25.5 kg

About: Galarians favour the distinctive aroma that drifts from this Pokémon's leaves. There's a popular perfume made using that scent.

GALARIAN LINOONE

Dark • Normal
0.5 m
32.5 kg

About: It uses its long tongue to taunt opponents. Once the opposition is enraged, this Pokémon hurls itself at the opponent, tackling them forcefully.

LUCARIO

Fighting • Steel
1.2 m
54.0 kg

About: It can tell what people are thinking. Only Trainers who have justice in their hearts can earn this Pokémon's trust.

MACHAMP

Fighting
1.6 m
130.0 kg

About: With four arms that react more quickly than it can think, it can execute many punches at once.

MACHOKE

Fighting
1.5 m
70.5 kg

About: Its formidable body never gets tired. It helps people by doing work such as the moving of heavy goods.

MACHOP

Fighting
0.8 m
19.5 kg

About: Always brimming with power, it passes time by lifting boulders. Doing so makes it even stronger.

MAGIKARP

Water
0.9 m
10.0 kg

About: This weak and pathetic Pokémon gets easily pushed along rivers when there are strong currents.

MAREANIE

Poison • Water
0.4 m
8.0 kg

About: Unlike their Alolan counterparts, the Mareanie of the Galar region have not yet figured out that the branches of Corsola are delicious.

MEOWSTIC

Psychic
0.6 m
8.5 kg

About: Revealing the eyelike patterns on the insides of its ears will unleash its psychic powers. It normally keeps the patterns hidden, however.

GALARIAN MEOWTH

Steel
0.4 m
7.5 kg

About: Living with a savage, seafaring people has toughened this Pokémon's body so much that parts of it have turned to iron.

MILCERY

Fairy
0.2 m
0.3 kg

About: This Pokémon was born from sweet-smelling particles in the air. Its body is made of cream.

MILOTIC

Water
6.2 m
162.0 kg

About: Milotic has provided inspiration to many artists. It has even been referred to as the most beautiful Pokémon of all.

MIMIKYU

Ghost • Fairy
0.2 m
0.7 kg

About: It wears a rag fashioned into a Pikachu costume in an effort to look less scary. Unfortunately, the costume only makes it creepier.

MORGREM

Dark • Fairy
0.8 m
12.5 kg

About: With sly cunning, it tries to lure people into the woods. Some believe it to have the power to make crops grow.

MORPEKO

Electric • Dark
0.3 m
3.0 kg

About: As it eats the seeds stored up in its pocket-like pouches, this Pokémon is not just satisfying its constant hunger. It's also generating electricity.

GALARIAN MR. MIME

Ice • Psychic
1.4 m
56.8 kg

About: It can radiate chilliness from the bottoms of its feet. It'll spend the whole day tap-dancing on a frozen floor.

MR. RIME

Ice • Psychic
1.5 m
58.2 kg

About: Its amusing movements make it very popular. It releases its psychic power from the pattern on its belly.

MUNCHLAX

Normal
0.6 m
105.0 kg

About: Stuffing itself with vast amounts of food is its only concern. Whether the food is rotten or fresh, yummy or tasteless – it does not care.

NICKIT

Dark
0.6 m
8.9 kg

About: Aided by the soft pads on its feet, it silently raids the food stores of other Pokémon. It survives off its ill-gotten gains.

NINETALES

Fire
1.1 m
19.9 kg

About: It is said to live 1,000 years, and each of its tails is loaded with supernatural powers.

OBSTAGOON

Dark • Normal
1.6 m
46.0 kg

About: It evolved after experiencing numerous fights. While crossing its arms, it lets out a shout that would make any opponent flinch.

ONIX

Rock • Ground
8.8 m
210.0 kg

About: As it digs through the ground, it absorbs many hard objects. This is what makes its body so solid.

ORBEETLE

Bug • Psychic
0.4 m
40.8 kg

About: It's famous for its high level of intelligence, and the large size of its brain is proof that it also possesses immense psychic power.

PANCHAM

Fighting
0.6 m
8.0 kg

About: Wanting to make sure it's taken seriously, Pancham's always giving others a glare. But if it's not focusing, it ends up smiling.

PANGORO

Fighting • Dark
2.1 m
136.0 kg

About: Using its leaf, Pangoro can predict the moves of its opponents. It strikes with punches that can turn a dump truck into scrap with just one hit.

PELIPPER

Water • Flying
1.2 m
28.0 kg

About: It is a messenger of the skies, carrying small Pokémon and eggs to safety in its bill.

PERRSERKER

Steel
0.8 m
28.0 kg

About: What appears to be an iron helmet is actually hardened hair. This Pokémon lives for the thrill of battle.

PICHU

Electric
0.3 m
2.0 kg

About: Despite its small size, it can zap even adult humans. However, if it does so, it also surprises itself.

PIKACHU

Electric
0.4 m
6.0 kg

About: When Pikachu meet, they'll touch their tails together and exchange electricity through them as a form of greeting.

PINCURCHIN

Electric
0.3 m
1.0 kg

About: It feeds on seaweed, using its teeth to scrape it off rocks. Electric current flows from the tips of its spines.

POLTEAGEIST

Ghost
0.2 m
0.4 kg

About: Leaving leftover black tea unattended is asking for this Pokémon to come along and pour itself into it, turning the tea into a new Polteageist.

GALARIAN PONYTA

Psychic
1.0 m
30.0 kg

About: Its small horn hides a healing power. With a few rubs from this Pokémon's horn, any slight wound you have will be healed.

RABOOT

Fire
0.6 m
9.0 kg

About: Its thick and fluffy fur protects it from the cold and enables it to use hotter fire moves.

RAICHU

Electric
0.8 m
30.0 kg

About: Its long tail serves as a ground to protect itself from its own high-voltage power.

RALTS

Psychic • Fairy
0.4 m
6.6 kg

About: If its horns capture the warm feelings of people or Pokémon, its body warms up slightly.

GALARIAN RAPIDASH

Psychic • Fairy
1.7 m
80.0 kg

About: Brave and prideful, this Pokémon dashes airily through the forest, its steps aided by the psychic power stored in the fur on its fetlocks.

RHYDON

Ground • Rock
1.9 m
120.0 kg

About: It begins walking on its hind legs after Evolution. It can punch holes through boulders with its horn.

RHYHORN

Ground • Rock
1.0 m
115.0 kg

About: Strong, but not too bright, this Pokémon can shatter even a skyscraper with its charging tackles.

RHYPERIOR

Ground • Rock
2.4 m
282.8 kg

About: It can load up to three projectiles per arm into the holes in its hands. What launches out of those holes could be either rocks or Roggenrola.

RILLABOOM

Grass
2.1 m
90.0 kg

About: The one with the best drumming techniques becomes the boss of the troop. It has a gentle disposition and values harmony among its group.

RIOLU

Fighting
0.7 m
20.2 kg

About: It's exceedingly energetic, with enough stamina to keep running all through the night. Taking it for walks can be a challenging experience.

ROLYCOLY

Rock
0.3 m
12.0 kg

About: Most of its body has the same composition as coal. Fittingly, this Pokémon was first discovered in coal mines about 400 years ago.

ROOKIDEE

Flying
0.2 m
1.8 kg

About: It will bravely challenge any opponent, no matter how powerful. This Pokémon benefits from every battle – even a defeat increases its strength a bit.

RUFFLET

Normal • Flying
0.5 m
10.5 kg

About: A combative Pokémon, it's ready to pick a fight with anyone. It has talons that can crush hard berries.

RUNERIGUS

Ground • Ghost
1.6 m
66.6 kg

About: A powerful curse was woven into an ancient painting. After absorbing the spirit of a Yamask, the painting began to move.

SANDACONDA

Ground
3.8 m
65.5 kg

About: Its unique style of coiling allows it to blast sand out of its sand sac more efficiently.

SCORBUNNY

Fire
0.3 m
4.5 kg

About: A warm-up of running around gets fire energy coursing through this Pokémon's body. Once that happens, it's ready to fight at full power.

SILICOBRA

Ground
2.2 m
7.6 kg

About: It spews sand from its nostrils. While the enemy is blinded, it burrows into the ground to hide.

SINISTEA

Ghost
0.1 m
0.2 kg

About: This Pokémon is said to have been born when a lonely spirit possessed a cold, leftover cup of tea.

SIRFETCH'D

Fighting
0.8 m
117.0 kg

About: Only Farfetch'd that have survived many battles can attain this evolution. When this Pokémon's leek withers, it will retire from combat.

SIZZLIPEDE

Fire • Bug
0.7 m
1.0 kg

About: It stores flammable gas in its body and uses it to generate heat. The yellow sections on its belly get particularly hot.

SKWOVET

Normal
0.3 m
2.5 kg

About: Found throughout the Galar region, this Pokémon becomes uneasy if its cheeks are ever completely empty of berries.

SLIGGOO

Dragon
0.8 m
17.5 kg

About: The lump on its back contains its tiny brain. It thinks only of food and escaping its enemies.

SNEASEL

Dark • Ice
0.9 kg
28 kg

About: Its paws conceal sharp claws. If attacked, it suddenly extends the claws and startles its enemy.

SNOM

Ice • Bug
0.3 m
3.8 kg

About: It shows no mercy to any who desecrate fields and mountains. It will fly around on its icy wings, causing a blizzard to chase offenders away.

SNORLAX

Normal
2.1 m
460.0 kg

About: This Pokémon's stomach is so strong, even eating mouldy or rotten food will not affect it.

SOBBLE

Water
0.3 m
4.0 kg

About: When scared, this Pokémon cries. Its tears pack the chemical punch of 100 onions, and attackers won't be able to resist weeping.

STEELIX

Steel • Ground
9.2 m
400 kg

About: It is said that if an Onix lives for over 100 years, its composition changes to become diamond-like.

STONJOURNER

Rock
2.5 m
520.0 kg

About: It stands in grasslands, watching the sun's descent from zenith to horizon. This Pokémon has a talent for delivering dynamic kicks.

GALARIAN STUNFISK

Ground • Steel
0.7m
20.5 kg

About:
Living in mud with a high iron content has given it a strong steel body.

SWOOBAT

Psychic • Flying
0.4 m
2.1 kg

About: Emitting powerful sound waves tires it out. Afterwards, it won't be able to fly for a little while.

SYLVEON

Fairy
1.0 m
23.5 kg

About: There's a Galarian fairy tale that describes a beautiful Sylveon vanquishing a dreadful dragon Pokémon.

THIEVUL

Dark
1.2 m
19.9 kg

About: It secretly marks potential targets with a scent. By following the scent, it stalks its targets and steals from them when they least expect it.

THWACKEY

Grass
0.7 m
14.0 kg

About: The faster a Thwackey can beat out a rhythm with its two sticks, the more respect it wins from its peers.

TOGEPI

Fairy
0.3 m
1.5 kg

About: The shell seems to be filled with joy. It is said that it will share good luck when treated kindly.

TOGETIC

Fairy • Flying
0.6 m
3.2 kg

About: They say that it will appear before kindhearted, caring people and shower them with happiness.

TOXAPEX

Poison • Water
0.7 m
14.5 kg

About: To survive in the cold waters of Galar, this Pokémon forms a dome with its legs, enclosing its body so it can capture its own body heat.

TOXEL

Electric • Poison
0.4 m
11.0 kg

About: It stores poison in an internal poison sac and secretes that poison through its skin. If you touch this Pokémon, a tingling sensation follows.

UMBREON

Dark
1.0 m
27.0 kg

About: On the night of a full moon, or when it gets excited, the ring patterns on its body glow yellow.

VAPOREON

Water
1.0 m
29.0 kg

About: When Vaporeon's fins begin to vibrate, it is a sign that rain will come within a few hours.

VIKAVOLT

Bug • Electric
1.5 m
45.0 kg

About: If it carries a Charjabug to use as a spare battery, a flying Vikavolt can rapidly fire high-powered beams of electricity.

VULPIX

Fire
0.6 m
9.9 kg

About: While young, it has six gorgeous tails. When it grows, several new tails are sprouted.

WEAVILE

Dark • Ice
1.1 m
34.0 kg

About: They attack their quarry in packs. Prey as large as Mamoswine easily fall to the teamwork of a group of Weavile.

GALARIAN WEEZING

Poison • Fairy
1.1 m
34.0 kg

About: This Pokémon consumes particles that contaminate the air. Instead of leaving droppings, it expels clean air.

WOBBUFFET

Psychic
1.3 m
28.5 kg

About: It hates light and shock. If attacked, it inflates its body to pump up its counterstrike.

WOOBAT

Psychic • Flying
0.4 m
2.1 kg

About: While inside a cave, if you look up and see lots of heart-shaped marks lining the walls, it's evidence that Woobat live there.

WOOLOO

Normal
0.6 m
6.0 kg

About: Its curly fleece is such an effective cushion that this Pokémon could fall off a cliff and stand right back up at the bottom, unharmed.

GALARIAN YAMASK

Ground • Ghost
0.5 m
1.5 kg

About: It's said that this Pokémon was formed when an ancient clay tablet was drawn to a vengeful spirit.

YAMPER

Electric
0.3 m
13.5 kg

About: This Pokémon is very popular as a herding dog in the Galar region. As it runs, it generates electricity from the base of its tail.

ZACIAN *LEGENDARY*

Fairy • Steel
2.8 m
355.0 kg

About: Able to cut down anything with a single strike, it became known as the Fairy King's Sword, and it inspired awe in friend and foe alike.

GALARIAN ZIGZAGOON

Dark • Normal
0.4 m
17.5 kg

About: Thought to be the oldest form of Zigzagoon, it moves in zigzags and wreaks havoc upon its surroundings.

ZAMAZENTA *LEGENDARY*

Fighting • Steel
2.9 m
785.0 kg

About: Its ability to deflect any attack led to it being known as the Fighting Master's Shield. It was feared and respected by all.

ZWEILOUS

Dark • Dragon
1.4 m
50.0 kg

About: Their two heads will fight each other over a single piece of food. Zweilous are covered in scars even without battling others.

TRICKY TYPES

These ten peculiar Pokémon that appear in the Galar region all belong to a different type category. Unscramble the words to discover each Pokémon's type. Use the pictures as handy hints!

1 CHIPYCS

2 LESTE

3 YAFIR

4 CRICTEEL

5 SIONOP

6 HIGGINTF

7 RIEF

8 KRAD

9 TWEAR

10 STOGH

The answers are on page 69.

CHLOE'S MEMORY GAME

Chloe is remembering a fun day Pokémon hunting in the Galar region. Study the picture for 60 seconds, then turn the page and try to answer as many questions as you can.

CHLOE'S MEMORY GAME

1. Which Pokémon was hiding behind a tree?

2. What was Sirfetch'd holding?

3. Which Bug- and Flying-type Pokémon was in full flight?

4. How many Applin did you spot?

5. Which winged critter has come out from its cave?

6. Diglett or Dugtrio – which was pictured?

7. Name the Pokémon that was feeling Electric.

8. Which Bug-type creature was crawling on the forest floor?

The answers are on page 69.

WARNING! WARNING!

Professor Oak has heard that Team Rocket have landed in the Galar region and are out to cause trouble AGAIN! Decode the Professor's warning message to Ash to see what the villains are planning this time.

A	B	C	D	E	F	G	H	I	J	K	L	M

N	O	P	Q	R	S	T	U	V	W	X	Y	Z

The answers are on page 69.

HAUNTING SIGHT

Ever get the feeling you're not alone in the darkness? It's probably a Haunter, lurking in the shadows. Connect Haunter to the spooky shadow that's an exact match.

The answers are on page 69.

BEAT THE HEAT

Get set to play with fire, Trainer! Nine scorching Fire-types
are hiding in the grid below – their names read forwards,
backwards, up, down and diagonally.
Find them all . . . and fast!

ARCANINE   CHARMELEON   NINETALES
CHARIZARD   FLAREON   SCORBUNNY
CHARMANDER   GROWLITHE   VULPIX

WHO'S THAT POKÉMON?
Which fiery fighter is hiding at the centre of the grid?

A. Scorbunny ☐   B. Raboot ☐   C. Cinderace ☐

The answers are on page 69.

SETTLING THE SCORBUNNY

After Lugia brought Ash and Goh together, the boys became research assistants at Professor Cerise's lab, where they are beginning a new day!

One morning, Goh had made a discovery. He headed straight to the lab, with Ash and Pikachu chasing behind.

"Read this, Professor!" Goh called, waving his Rotom Phone. "It says that Pokémon can grow *GIANT-SIZED*."

"Woah!" said Ash. "That sounds totally awesome!"

Professor Cerise smiled. "You'll find those giant-sized Pokémon in the Galar region," he explained. "Perhaps it's time you saw them for yourselves?"

"ALL RIGHT!" cheered Ash and Goh.

And that's just what they did! Ash, Goh and Pikachu took a plane to the Galar region, travelling further from home than they ever had before. There was just time for a snack, before catching a train to their final destination, the Wild Area.

Pikachu and the boys couldn't get enough of the delicious scones – a Galar region speciality! Full at last, Ash placed the leftover scones in his backpack.

Seconds later, from out of nowhere, a stone came flying through the air. Then a Pokémon appeared. Its ears were long and its fur was scruffy and brown.

"Quick! Grab your camera," Ash told Goh. But as they scrambled to find their Rotom Phones, a pack of Nickit scampered in and swiped Ash's backpack! The bunny-like Pokémon hopped after the thieves.

Ash, Goh and Pikachu quickly gave chase – their train tickets were inside the backpack! But when they turned the corner, the Nickit had vanished.

"Where did they go?" Ash panted.

Suddenly, a second stone sailed through the air, landing neatly on the bell of a parked bicycle. *DING!* Ash and Goh turned to see who had thrown it. It was the same brazen bunny as before!

"SCOR!" it sneered.

"It's a decoy – the Nickit are getting further away!" warned Goh.

Ash and Goh split up. Goh followed a trail of footprints, while Ash and Pikachu took a wrong turn.

A *dead end*? No way!" Ash cried.

He and Pikachu trudged back the way they had come, to find Goh. They soon tracked him down – hiding behind a bush. He was watching the Nickit and the Pokémon thief search the backpack.

"Let's see what they do next," whispered Goh. He quickly scanned the group of Pokémon with his Rotom Phone.

"NICKIT . . . the Fox Pokémon," bleeped Rotom. "Nickit steals food that other Pokémon have found. It erases any footprints it leaves behind with its fluffy tail."

Goh tried to scan the taller Pokémon next, but no data was found!

"Does that mean . . ." said Goh.

"We've found a *NEW SPECIES*!" said Ash.

The Pokémon gave each Nickit a piece of scone, saving one bit for itself. But the Nickit growled, hungrily wanting more! Goh and Ash watched as the Pokémon then shared its own piece of scone.

"It's a good friend to those Nickit," said Goh.
"Sharing with friends is what it's all about," Ash replied. "But those tasty things and that backpack belong to *ME*!"
He leapt out from behind the bush, startling the critters, but the tall Pokémon threw the backpack out of Ash's reach. Then the Pokémon aimed a flying leap his way. Pikachu sprang to his buddy's defence.

"Pikachu, use *IRON TAIL*!" Ash called. The Pokémon then took on Pikachu using some smart moves of its own! The pair were locked in battle – which Pokémon would come out on top?

"*ELECTRO WEB*!" Ash commanded next. This time, Pikachu's mega move trapped the Pokémon in a powerful web of electric beams. The Pokémon was stunned at last!

"We did it, Pikachu!" Ash smiled.

"*PIKA! PIKA!*" Pikachu squeaked back.

Ash moved closer to the defeated Pokémon. "You're a lot of fun!" he smiled.

But it was in no mood to make friends . . . instead, the furball flattened Ash with another flying kick!

"That was some move!" said Goh, impressed.

It raised its paw to its mouth and giggled. As it did so, a patch of white appeared on the Pokémon's furry face. Goh was puzzled.

Suddenly, the Nickit ran past again, with the café owner hot on their heels – the greedy gang had stolen more treats! Soon, the man had them cornered. The Nickit began to tremble, until the furry Pokémon hopped in to help!

"You again," said the café owner, holding up the Pokémon. "It's time you stopped your trickery."

"Mister, *WAIT*!" a voice called. It was Goh! "I'm very sorry," he began. "The truth is, that's my Pokémon!"

The man let go of the creature. "Your Pokémon?" he said, surprised.

"Yes, sir," Goh replied. "I'll make sure it never steals again," he promised.

Everyone headed back to the café. Goh couldn't bear to see the Pokémon go hungry, so he ordered them a large plate of scones.

The café owner smiled. "Why did you tell a fib earlier?" he asked Goh.

"How did you know?" said Goh, shocked.

"It was the look on Scorbunny's face when you said it belonged to you," the man replied.

Goh scratched his head. "Scorbunny? That's what it's called?" he said.

"Why, of course!" the café owner smiled.

"Rotom . . ." Goh said. "Show me the data for Scorbunny."

"Scorbunny," the Rotom bleeped back. "The Rabbit Pokémon. A Fire type. The pads on the soles of its feet are said to bring good luck."

Ash studied the screen. "It's supposed to be white," he said, puzzled. "But that Scorbunny is **BROWN**."

"It covers itself in mud," the café owner explained. He told the boys all about how a muddy Scorbunny had arrived long ago in the town, and how it helps the hungry Nickit to find food. "Scorbunny takes nothing in return," the man said.

Goh felt sorry for Scorbunny and knelt down beside it. "It's a big world out there," he said kindly. "Anywhere you want to go, you can just go! You'll make all sorts of friends!"

"And those kicks of yours will always get you out of trouble!" Goh went on.

Scorbunny smiled. It was about to launch another kick at Ash, when Goh saw the time.

"**QUICK!**" he yelled. "Our train leaves in five minutes!"

They grabbed their things and sprinted to the station. Scorbunny sighed as the boys disappeared out of sight. The Nickit knew what they had to do. Thanks to Scorbunny, they were now ready to make their own way in the world. So they scooped up Scorbunny and chased after Ash, Goh and Pikachu. They didn't stop until they had safely delivered their friend on to the train. Then the Nickit turned and shook their furry tails to bid Scorbunny farewell.

As the train pulled out of the station moments later, Ash and Goh had no idea that Scorbunny had boarded the train. They were busy telling the professors all about the new Pokémon they had discovered.

"Scorbunny's amazing!" Goh told Professor Cerise. "It covered itself in mud to look like the Nickit! That's why my Rotom Phone didn't recognise it at first."

"Could be," said Professor Cerise. "Thank you for sharing your fascinating story with us – and stay safe in the Wild Area."

"*We will!*" said Goh and Ash together, before hanging up.

Just then, a rumbling noise came from Pikachu's tummy.

Ash groaned. "I'm as hungry as you, Pikachu!"

Pikachu searched in Ash's backpack, but only crumbs from the scones remained. So imagine their surprise when Goh pulled out a fresh bag of treats from his own backpack!

"A present from the café owner!" he announced. "*LET'S EAT!*"

The first Pokémon Ash and Goh met in Galar was Scorbunny, a curious creature who can be hot to handle! Where will our heroes' adventures take them next? Join them, as their journey continues!

SETTLING THE SCORBUNNY

The following questions are all based on the story of when Ash and Goh first met Scorbunny. Choose to play as Ash or Goh, then go head-to-head with another Trainer to see who comes out on top.

For a tougher test, tackle all ten questions yourself!

PLAYER 1: ASH

1 What did Scorbunny use to disguise himself?

2 Which treat from Galar did Ash and Goh buy at the café?

3 Which part of Scorbunny's body is considered to be lucky?

4 What device does Goh use to find data on new Pokémon?

5 How do Nickit get their food?

SCORE:

58

PLAYER 2: GOH

1 *To which area in the Galar region are Ash and Goh travelling?*

---

2 *What type of Pokémon is Scorbunny?*

---

3 *What is the name of the head professor at the laboratory in the Kanto region?*

---

4 *Which two moves did Pikachu use to stun Scorbunny?*

---

5 *What is Nickit also known as?*

SCORE:

Check the answers, then enter your scores!

The answers are on page 69.

SWEET TREAT

Goh has a sweet snack for Scorbunny, but which berry is its favourite? Trace the letters on the right path to find out.

The answers are on page 69.

CAVE CHALLENGE

Which cave-dwelling critters are all in a flutter? Put the picture back in the correct order to reveal the Pokémon!

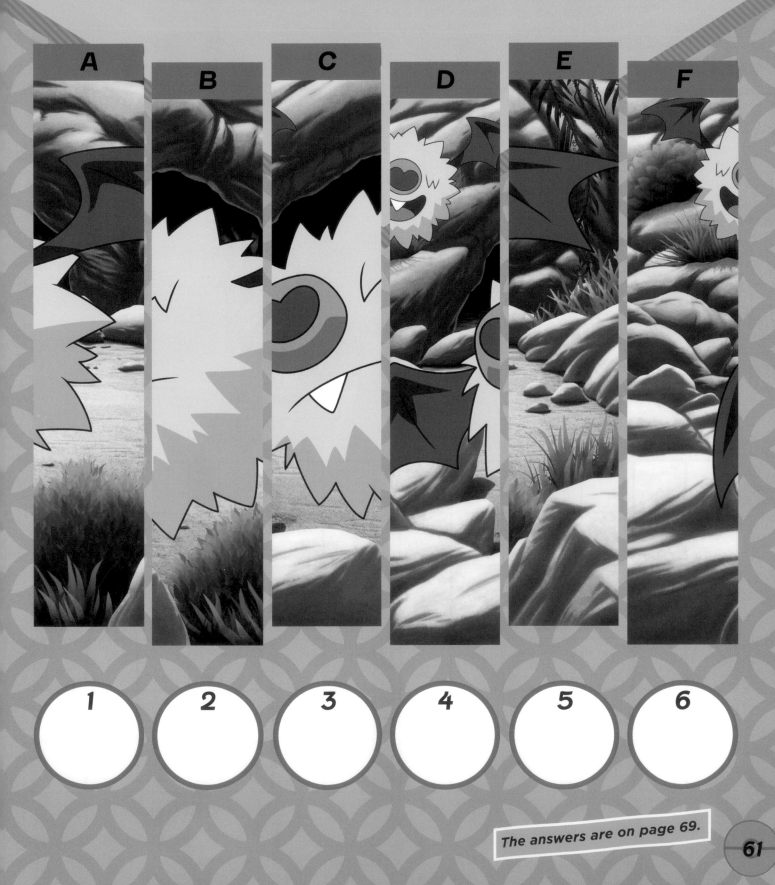

1   2   3   4   5   6

The answers are on page 69.

TIC-TAC-HO!

Ash has always wanted to battle Ho-Oh, while Goh wants to add the Legendary bird to his Pokédex! Take on another Trainer in this one-on-one game.

PLAYER 1	PLAYER 2

HOW TO PLAY:

Decide who will play as H and who will play as O. Take turns writing your letters in the spaces on the grid until one player has made a row of three of their letters. If all nine spaces are filled with no winner, it's a draw. Remember to keep score!

EEVEE'S EVOLUTIONS

Eevee may be a Normal-type Pokémon but it's hard to find a more special creature! How many of Eevee's evolved forms do you know? Fill in their names below.

The answers are on page 69.

SLEEPING WARRIOR

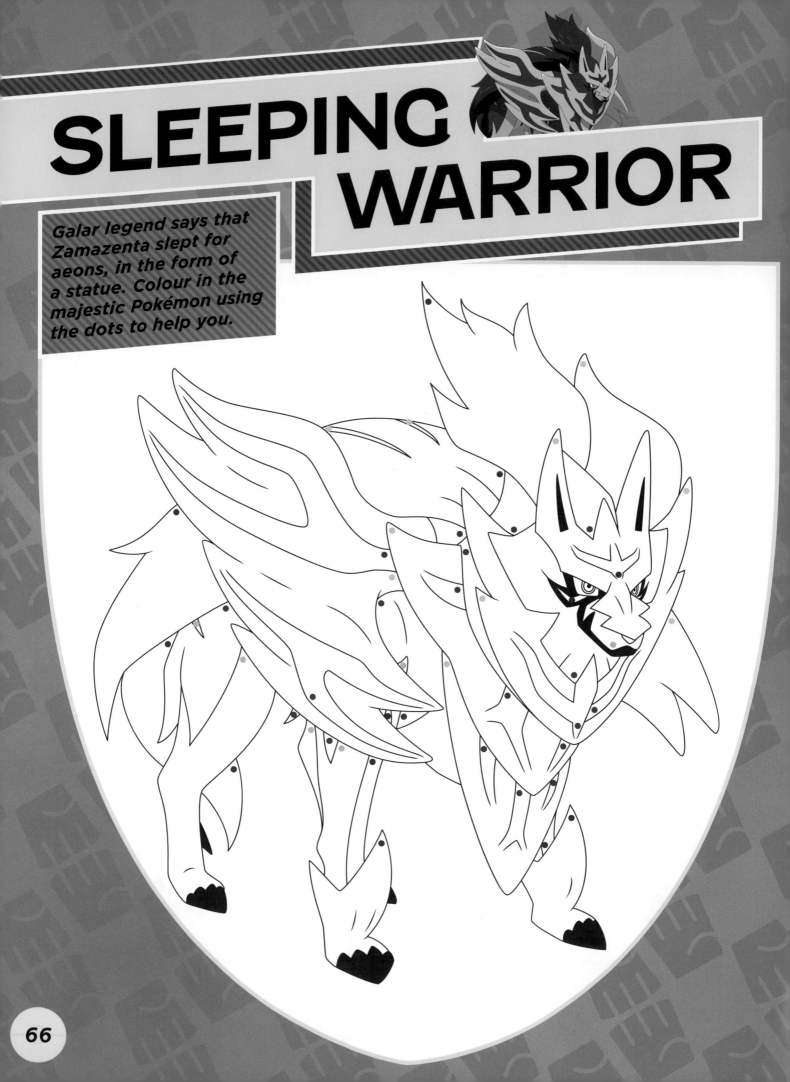

Galar legend says that Zamazenta slept for aeons, in the form of a statue. Colour in the majestic Pokémon using the dots to help you.

FILLING THE DEX

Trying to complete his Galar Pokédex is starting to bug Goh! Help him by drawing lines to connect the names of the Bug-type Pokémon to their pictures.

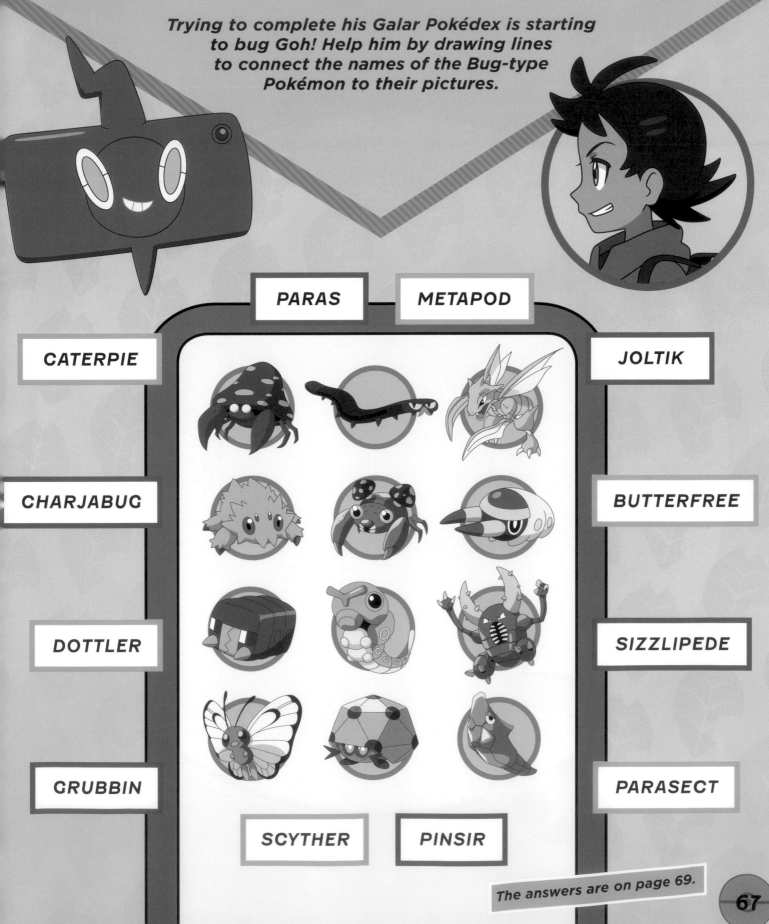

PARAS

METAPOD

CATERPIE

JOLTIK

CHARJABUG

BUTTERFREE

DOTTLER

SIZZLIPEDE

GRUBBIN

PARASECT

SCYTHER

PINSIR

The answers are on page 69.

I CHOOSE YOU!

If you had to buddy up with just one Pokémon from the Galar region, who would you pick? Draw your perfect partner in the Poké Ball.

ANSWERS

Page 9 SPOT THE DIFFERENCE

Page 10 BRIGHT SPARK

The Pokémon is YAMPER.

Page 11 ON THE GOH!

Page 12 PERFECT POKÉ BALLS

Dive Ball – Greninja; Net Ball – Butterfree; Master Ball – Mew; Dusk Ball – Gengar.

Page 13 FIRING UP

The Pokémon is CHARIZARD.

Page 24 THE PROFESSOR'S QUIZ

1. Legendary; 2. Flying- & Psychic-type Pokémon; 3. Yes; 4. No; 5. 5.2 m; 6. Its wings.

Page 25 STRANGE SIGHTING

Page 26 GALAR DISCOVERIES

Page 42 TRICKY TYPES

1. PSYCHIC, 2. STEEL, 3. FAIRY, 4. ELECTRIC, 5. POISON, 6. FIGHTING, 7. FIRE, 8. DARK, 9. WATER, 10. GHOST.

Pages 43–44 CHLOE'S MEMORY GAME

1. Larvitar; 2. A leek; 3. Butterfree; 4. Four; 5. Woobat; 6. Dugtrio; 7. Yamper; 8. Grubbin.

Page 45 WARNING! WARNING!

Professor Oak's message reads: ASH, TAKE EXTRA CARE . . . TEAM ROCKET HAVE RECRUITED A DITTO TO TRY TO CAPTURE PIKACHU.

Page 46 HAUNTING SIGHT

Shadow D matches Haunter.

Page 47 FIERY FIENDS

WHO'S THAT POKÉMON? *B – Raboot.*

Page 58 SETTLING THE SCORBUNNY QUIZ!

Player 1: ASH
1. Mud; 2. Scones; 3. The soles of its feet (also its nose); 4. Rotom Phone; 5. Other Pokémon steal it for them.

Player 2: GOH
1. The Wild Area; 2. A Fire-type Pokémon; 3. Professor Cerise; 4. Iron Tail and Electro Web; 5. The Fox Pokémon.

Page 60 SWEET TREAT

PINAP BERRY.

Page 61 CAVE CHALLENGE

1. F, 2. D, 3. C, 4. B, 5. A, 6. E.

Page 65 EEVEE'S EVOLUTIONS

Page 67 FILLING THE DEX

PARASECT	SIZZLIPEDE	SCYTHER
JOLTIK	PARAS	GRUBBIN
CHARJABUG	CATERPIE	PINSIR
BUTTERFREE	DOTTLER	METAPOD